D0981418

OTHER YEARLING BOOKS YOU WILL ENJOY:

YEARLING BOOKS are designed especially to entertain and enlighten young people. Charles F. Reasoner, Professor Emeritus of Children's Literature and Reading, New York University, is consultant to this series.

For a complete listing of all Yearling titles, write to Promotion Department, Dell Publishing Co., Inc., P.O. Box 3000, Pine Brook, N.J. 07058.

A GIRL CALLED AL

by CONSTANCE C. GREENE

Illustrated by Byron Barton

A YEARLING BOOK

Published by
Dell Publishing Co., Inc.
1 Dag Hammarskjold Plaza
New York, New York 10017

Yearling ® TM 913705, Dell Publishing Co., Inc.

ISBN: 0-440-42810-6

This edition published
by arrangement with The Viking Press, Inc.
Printed in the United States of America
September 1977

10
CW

*To Sheppard, Philippa,
Stephanie, Matthew, and Lucia*

A Girl Called Al

ABOUT THIS BOOK

There's a new girl down the hall from us. She said, "Call me Al," and it wasn't until I saw her report card that I found out her name is Alexandra. Al is a little on the fat side and the only girl in the whole school, practically, with pigtails. "I am a nonconformist," she says like she was saying she was Elizabeth Taylor or something. Her parents are divorced, but she says she doesn't mind: she gets more presents that way.

This is the beginning of a warm, utterly real story of the friendship between two girls in a city apartment house.

ALA Notable Book

There's a new girl moved down the hall from us. She said "Call me Al" and it wasn't until I saw her report card that I found out her name was Alexandra. She hates it.

She has lived in a lot of different places. She has lived on the Coast, among other places. In L.A.

"I have never heard of Ellay," I said. "Where is that?"

Al explained to me that L.A. is short for Los Angeles. In California. They have a lot of smog there.

She has been on an airplane a lot of times. She said the next time she goes on one she will bring me one of the little plastic dishes of jelly and stuff they give you.

I have never been on an airplane.

She has been to Hollywood where she saw them making a movie. "It's not so much," she said.

She has Doris Day's autograph.

"And that dopey guy who always plays with her. He's such a dope he makes me sick. What does she see in a dope like that?" Al said.

She has been to Disneyland about a thousand times.

"It's not so much," she said.

Al is a little on the fat side, which is why I didn't like her right at first. That's not fair, I know. She might not like me because I'm on the skinny side. To each his own, my father says. But it wasn't just because of that. She walks stiff, like a German soldier, and she has pigtails. She is the only girl in the whole entire school, practically, with pigtails. They would make her stand out even if nothing else did. Most of the kids have long, straight hair like mine. My father says I remind him of a sheep dog but I don't care. Al's pigtails look like they are starched. She does not smile a lot and she wears glasses. Her teeth are very nice, though, and she does not wear braces. Most kids I know have to wear braces. They are very expensive and also a pain in the neck. I am fortunate, my father says, because I have inherited my teeth from his side of the family. It saves him a pile of dough, he says. My brother inherited his teeth from my mother's side, I guess. He has a retainer and all that stuff.

Al is a very interesting person. She is a year older than me but we're both in the seventh grade, on account of she dropped back when she moved here. She has gone to a lot of different schools. She has a very high I.Q., she says, but she doesn't work to capacity. She says things like this all the time but I don't like to let on I don't always know what she is talking about.

"I am a nonconformist," she said, like she was saying she was a television star or Elizabeth Taylor or something.

"What's that mean?" Here I go again.

"It means I don't follow the herd. It's the best way to be. You," she said, looking over the top of her glasses at me, "have the makings of a nonconformist. There's a lot of work to be done, but I think maybe we can manage."

Most of the things Al and I talk about I don't tell my mother. She probably wouldn't get them. The first night Al moved into the building, her mother came to our door. She had a mess of green stuff on her eyelids, and her fingernails looked about two inches long.

She said, "I wonder if you'd be good enough to let me use your telephone. Mine has not as yet been installed. I will reimburse you, of course."

She's not my mother's cup of tea, whatever that means. My mother says she likes most people, but I've noticed that when you come right down to it there are a lot of people she doesn't like.

She's very critical, my mother.

Al's mother works. She's got a very important job in a department store downtown. When she comes home at night her feet hurt and she takes a tub. That's what she says. She doesn't take a bath, she takes a tub. When I was there the first time, she came in, and after Al introduced us she said she had to run and take a tub. I guess I looked funny because Al said, "She means a bath."

"What's the difference?" I asked.

"A tub has all kinds of gunk in it," Al said. "Like bath salts and bath oil and things like that."

My mother takes mostly baths.

Al says she doesn't love her mother that much. I never heard anyone say they didn't love their mother before. She likes her because she's her mother, she says. She respects her, but she doesn't love her that much. She loves her father. He sends her salt-water taffy from Atlantic City when he is at a convention, or a couple of jumping beans from Mexico when he is at another convention.

Al's mother and father are divorced. She says she doesn't mind too much that they are divorced. She gets more presents that way. She has a picture of her father over her bureau. She says he is very handsome and smart.

My father is not very tall and he is going bald. Every year at my birthday he pretends he can't remember how old I am. He always takes off a year or two. Practically the only time he gets mad at me is when I bring home D's on my report card.

"You can do better," he says.

I wonder what my I.Q. is and if I am working up to my capacity.

Chapter Two

Our home-room teacher, Mr. Keogh, is the only teacher in the whole school who calls Al "Al." All the others call her Alexandra and she turns about eight colors of the rainbow. I said it to myself under my breath and it sounded pretty. But you know how kids are about their own names. Even if they really like them, they pretend they don't.

Al doesn't want to take cooking and sewing. She wants to take shop. But in our school only boys get to take shop, and when Al told Mr. Keogh about this he said he would talk to the principal but not to hold out too much hope.

Al and Mr. Keogh are friends. She talks to him before class. She found out Mr. Keogh's wife was having an operation.

"It's so sad," she said. "I feel so sorry for Mr. Keogh. His wife is having an operation."

I wondered about Mr. Keogh's wife. I feel sorry for *her*. She's the one who's having the operation.

"What's the matter with her?"

"She has ball stones," Al said.

"What?" I said. "I have never heard of ball stones."

"She has ball stones," Al said like she was an authority on the subject. "You know. In her gladder."

It must be so if Al says so. I am not up on operations.

Except for taking out tonsils. It is supposed to be a breeze. Everyone is very jolly, saying ho ho, what fun it will be. Just think. You will get ice cream and ginger ale whenever you want. Won't that be fun? What a blast.

Mr. Keogh came back after lunch and said he had talked to the principal and the principal said that Al cannot take shop. It is against the rules, he said. She will have to take cooking the first half of the year and sewing the second half, like all the other girls.

"Why don't they make up a new set of rules?" Al wanted to know. "I bet they never had a girl before who wanted to take shop. I want to make a bookshelf like those guys are making. I don't want to learn how to sew a dumb old skirt or make a mess of muffins."

Al was mad as anything and she marched out of the room and her pigtails were swinging like someone was hanging on to the ends of them.

"Why can't she take shop if she wants to?" I asked. "What's the harm?"

Mr. Keogh had on his blue polka-dot tie today. That meant it was Tuesday. He wears a red one for Monday and a green one for Wednesday and switches around for the rest of the week.

"You can't fight city hall," he said.

It's another one of those things people say, like, "I'm from Missouri," which is what my father says when my mother says she's going to budget her food money so we can eat out once a month on what she saves.

I happen to know my father is from Chicago, Illinois.

So there you are.

Anyway, I could see that Mr. Keogh felt pretty bad about Al not being able to take shop and make a bookshelf.

"Maybe her father can help her at home," he said to me. "All it takes is a saw and a couple of pieces of wood."

"Al's father is usually in Atlantic City or Mexico at a convention," I explained. "He is divorced."

"Oh," said Mr. Keogh. "I didn't know that. I'm sorry. That is too bad. Well."

Al came back into the room and she was walking

just as straight and mad as before. "Suppose I say I won't take dumb old cooking and sewing. What then?"

Mr. Keogh sat on the edge of his desk and tugged at his ear, which Al has pointed out to me usually means he doesn't know what he is going to say next.

"They'd probably make you take an extra math course," he said. "To fill in the time."

Math is Al's worst subject.

"Mr. Keogh," I said, "I'm sorry to hear about your wife's ball stones."

Mr. Keogh looked like he'd had a hard day.

"What?" he said.

"Your wife. I'm sorry she has ball stones."

"Oh, yes," Mr. Keogh said, and he put on his hat and went home.

Chapter Three

"Will you take a load of stuff and put it in the washing machine for me?" my mother asked.

It was Saturday morning. Our machine is on the blink and she doesn't want to buy a new one this month.

"It never rains but it pours," she says. Our car has to have a new differential, whatever that is, and my brother Teddy went to the orthodontist last week and he has to wear his braces another year.

"Sure," I said. I was glad. I would get a chance to visit Mr. Richards. He is sort of the assistant superintendent of our building. He makes change for people for the washers and dryers, and fixes leaky faucets, and once in a while, he shovels snow.

We have been friends for quite a while. He is a retired bartender and has a big tattoo on his arm that says "Home Sweet Home." I had been wanting to have Al meet him. We figured out night before last that Al and I have known each other for exactly three weeks. It feels like forever. Some people you just feel like you have always known. That is the way it is with me and Al and with me and Mr. Richards.

He has the cleanest, shiniest kitchen floor I have ever seen. You can practically see your face in it. Nobody but me knows how he gets it that way. It is one of the things that makes him so special.

I rang Al's bell, but softly. I gave it just a little poke. Her mother has to do a lot of traveling and entertaining, as she is the buyer for Better Dresses, and you never know when she has maybe got in at one o'clock in the morning or something. She wears a sleep shade for her eyes and plugs for her ears. Al showed them to me but sometimes, even all stuffed up with all those things, she can still hear the bell.

Al came to the door and she did not have her hair in pigtails yet. It looked nice.

"I like your hair that way," I said. "Why not wear it to school like that?"

"It's a mess," she said. Without her glasses and her hair in pigtails, she looked different.

"I've got to go down and put some clothes in the washing machine," I whispered, just in case. "Come with me and we'll go see Mr. Richards."

She said, "In a sec," and when she came back she looked the way she does every day. It was a disappointment.

"Pleased to meet you," Mr. Richards said to Al. They shook hands and he asked, "Got time for a little shooter of Coke?"

I had just finished telling Al he talks this way on account of being a retired bartender, so it was nice he proved I wasn't making it up.

His apartment is right behind the furnace room, so it is always warm. "You in the building?" he asked Al, putting out the glasses. "Set 'em up," he said and slid three glasses down the kitchen counter.

"She's new," I said. "She's in 14-C."

"You got enough heat up there in 14-C?" Mr. Richards wanted to know. "We had plenty of problems with that one, I can tell you. Last tenant said it got so cold he didn't need the refrigerator. Just left everything out on the table. Care for another?"

We all had another shooter. I never used to like Coke until I started drinking it this way.

"Don't worry," Al said. "You don't know my mother. She would not hesitate to let you know the minute anything was not right."

I think Mr. Richards's eyes are blue. They are so narrow in his face it is hard to tell. I told him once that I thought he looked like the captain of a whaling ship. I could see him squinting out over the horizon. "Not me," he had said. "Them waves get to my stomach every time."

"You have a nice place here," Al said.

Al is a very observant girl. She says if she does not get to be a specialist in internal medicine, she may be a newspaper reporter. I would not put it past her.

"I like your curtains," she said, "and that's a pretty plant. What kind is it?"

"That's a geranium," Mr. Richards said, looking pleased. "I been treating it like a baby, better'n most babies, if you want to know. Lots of sun, not too much water. Some day maybe, when my ship comes in, when I find that there pot of gold, when I break the bank at that place they wrote the song about, I'll move where it's warm. All the time. I'll get me a house with nothing but flowers and plants around. No grass, no nothing. Just flowers and plants."

Mr. Richards was really getting carried away. He tied a couple of rags around his sneakers and started skating around his linoleum.

I was very pleased. I had told Al he skated around his floor when he got excited. Or sometimes just for fun. It relaxes him, he says.

She only said, "I don't believe it."

One thing about Al, she never comes right out and calls anyone a liar.

Now I just smiled at her. I wanted to say, "I told you so," but I didn't. Which I thought was kind of nice of me.

Chapter Four

"I like your lady friend," Mr. Richards said the next day when I took a bunch of towels down to the dryer for my mother. I had stopped at Al's to ask her to come along, but she had said, "My mother has a rule. She says we have to spend Sundays together. She says she doesn't see enough of me during the week." She made a face. So I went alone.

"She's a humdinger," Mr. Richards said. "A regular lollapalooza."

My mother has a thing about me visiting him. It's not just that he's a retired bartender. My mother takes a drink now and then. It's mainly because whenever she sees him around, he's always got a toothpick sticking out of his mouth. He is almost never without a toothpick. She thinks it's common. It makes *me* nervous. Some day he will swallow it. Or get a big hole in his gums.

Anyway, she thinks the combination does not make for a very good companion for me. She doesn't really know Mr. Richards.

"I like that Al," Mr. Richards said, fixing me a piece of bread and butter and sugar. He didn't even ask if I wanted it. He slapped on the butter and put about ten inches of sugar on top. My mother would have exploded.

"Al is a very interesting person," I said. "She is a nonconformist."

"That so?"

One thing about Mr. Richards, he is a very good listener. I mean, he really hears you and he never interrupts.

"You probably won't believe this," I said, biting into my second piece of bread, "but Al wants to take shop instead of sewing and cooking, and they won't let her."

"Who won't let her?" Mr. Richards asked.

"The principal, that's who. No girls get to take shop."

Mr. Richards scratched his head. "Seems like a perfectly normal thing. A young lady wants to take shop, then I say let her take shop. A girl like Al, she doesn't want to waste her time with ladylike pursuits She wants to get out and live life, change a tire or two, cut down a few trees."

Mr. Richards was warming up. He started to skate. He tied his rags on and off he went.

"Why, she wants to scale a couple of mountains, dig for buried treasure, sail to the South Seas in a twenty-foot sloop. Stuff like that."

He glided around nice and easy and after five minutes the floor gleamed and he wasn't even out of breath.

"You think it would do any good if I went down to this here school and talked to the principal?" he asked.

I figured he might do more harm than good, so I said, "No, no, that wouldn't be such a good idea. The only thing is, Al wants to make a bookshelf like the guys in shop are making."

"Well now," he said, putting on the pot for soup, "that's all they're doing? That's not so much."

When Mr. Richards makes soup it is something to watch. He keeps a bag of stuff in his refrigerator. Like celery tops and old bones and carrots and onions. If it's around holidays, he throws in the leftover turkey. Then he scrapes plates and if there's any spinach or mashed potatoes or salad left, he throws it all in.

I nearly got sick the first time I saw him do it. It looked pretty disgusting. Then I ate some once when

he hadn't told me he had made it and it was the best soup I ever ate. I don't exactly know how to describe it, but it was delicious.

"I could teach her how to make a bookshelf," he said, pouring salt into the pot, "if her daddy isn't handy. I'm no slouch with the tools. I got a hammer, some nails lying around somewhere. I might just hunt them up and teach both you young ladies a thing or two."

"Her daddy isn't around," I said. "He is divorced from her mother. He travels a lot."

"Well," said Mr. Richards, "then we will do it."

Another thing about him. He doesn't say he's going to do something and then forget it. Like lots of people do. Mostly grownups.

He never says, "Some other time." He never says that. He does what he says he's going to do.

He is really very refreshing.

Chapter Five

"I think Mr. Richards must have been quite handsome when he was a young man," Al said when I told her he was going to help us make a bookshelf starting next Saturday morning. "If it doesn't snow, that is. If it snows, Mr. Richards will have to clean the walks."

Mr. Richards is practically my best friend, outside of Al, but I do not think he was ever what you would call handsome.

"He has great character in his face," Al said. "And his ears are lovely and close to his head."

I had never noticed his ears but I made a mental note to check them the next time I saw him.

Al is saving up for contact lenses.

"My mother wears contact lenses," she said. "She's in Better Dresses, you know, and they like the people in Better Dresses to be chic. And it makes a world of difference when she has to wear a hat or go to a formal affair. In an evening gown."

I can't see Al in either a hat or an evening gown. But that is beside the point.

"Next time you come over, you can watch her," Al said.

"Watch her what?" I asked. I have only seen Al's mother a couple of times, outside of the first day they moved in. I do not think she knows my name.

"Watch her slip the lenses in and out," she said. "It's very interesting. That is, if it doesn't make you nervous."

Al stopped and tightened one pigtail. She likes them neat and even. Those pigtails are her badge of nonconformity, she says. She may be right.

"Why would it make me nervous?" I asked.

"There's only one thing," she said. "Can't you guess? Take a good guess. What would be the most logical thing that could go wrong?"

She sat with her hands on her knees and I knew she was trying to see inside my head to see how my brain works. She made a noise like *zzt zzt*, which meant she was X-raying my head.

"Figure it out by logic," she said.

Al says I have a block about logic, that I reject it.

That means I am no good at it. My father says that women are not logical by nature.

Al watched me without blinking, like a little baby. Little babies or real little kids can look at you for a long time without blinking. One time in church there was a little kid sitting in front of me and I tried to stare him down about a hundred times. He won every time.

"I have a cramp in my foot," I said. I got up and jumped around. When I finished she was still watching me.

"I don't know," is what I came up with.

Al snorted.

"Just think," she said, "what would happen if she whipped them in and all of a sudden something went wrong and they kept on going. I mean, where would they end up?"

"On the floor?" I knew this was not the right answer.

Al sighed and closed her eyes. She had lost her patience. She loses her patience often but she is quiet about it. When my mother loses her patience, she tells everybody.

Al sucked in her cheeks. She practices sucking in her cheeks for ten minutes every day. It makes her look very old. It really does the trick. She looks about forty or forty-two.

"I'll tell you where they end up. I'll just tell you!" She started waving her arms around. Then she stopped and said she had to go to the bathroom. I have noticed that she frequently has to go to the bathroom when she is in the middle of a story. I guess the excitement is too much for her.

"Where was I?" she said when she came back.

"Where do the contacts end up when something goes wrong," I said.

"Oh, yes. Well, I'm going to tell you."

One thing about Al is you cannot rush her when she is telling a story.

Softly she said, "First, they slide down inside your cheek and wiggle around in your throat. Then," she said, "then . . ."

She is like Mr. Keogh when he tugs at his ear because he doesn't know what he's going to say next. Only she squints up at the ceiling, like maybe there is something written there. Finally she looked at me and smiled.

"Then they slip down inside your stomach and into the large intestine."

I have never been sure of the difference between

the large intestine and the small intestine. They are different in size is all I know.

She looked at the ceiling and then at me. "Then you know where they go?"

I racked my brains to remember the diagram of the stomach we have on the wall in biology class. It is a mess. I do not like that kind of thing. I would make a lousy nurse.

"I'll tell you," Al shouted, hopping around on one foot. "They slide right down your legs and into your feet and there is one contact in your left foot and one in your right. All of a sudden you're walking around on glass. That's all!"

Al was exhausted. She sank back into her chair.

"Don't you think you'd better warn your mother?" I asked her.

Chapter Six

"Can I have my friend Al for supper?" I asked my mother, on account of she was whistling, which she only does when she is in a good mood, and also we were having spaghetti and meat balls, which I know is absolutely Al's favorite food.

"Tonight?" she said. "A school night?"

I explained that Al was going to be alone. Her mother had a dinner engagement. My mother started to say something and then she dropped a meat ball on the floor. She bent over and picked it up and rinsed it off.

"Waste not, want not," she said and threw it back in the pot. "Remember that, with the price of food what it is today. Your father works too hard to get the money to pay the bills."

All this is true, if beside the point. All I asked was could I have my friend Al for supper.

"Mom," I said, "you are a good woman."

This usually gets to her.

"Get me the sugar, like a good girl, will you?" she said. Then she added a little of it, tasted the sauce, and added, "Yes, I guess Al can come for supper tonight. Put another place on the table."

I ran down the hall to tell Al she could come. I had already told her I thought it would be all right and she'd said, "My mother left me a turkey potpie in the freezer and a whole quart of ice cream. Butter pecan. Maybe you can come and eat with me."

The door opened before I even had a chance to ring.

"Come on over," I said, out of breath. "We're eating the minute my father gets home because it's his bowling night. We're having spaghetti. And garlic bread."

"Wait," she said. "I've got to comb my hair. It's a mess."

"You look fine," I said.

Al changed her skirt and put on a blue sweater that I had not seen before.

"Is that a present from your father?" I said.

"Are you kidding? My father never gives me clothes. It's from my mother. She picked it up on sale at the store. My mother buys all my clothes on sale. She gets the employee discount." Al braided her hair while she held her rubber bands between her teeth.

"Come on, we'll be late."

"And who is this young lady?" my father said when we came to our apartment. He has only met Al about fifty times, but every time he gets up and shakes her hand and says the same thing.

She thinks he's a riot.

"All right," my mother said and my brother Teddy practically knocked us over to get to the table first. He is nine. He is very good in science. He plans to go to M.I.T. and be a bachelor when he grows up. My father says that is all right with him, but Teddy better plan on getting a scholarship.

"Lord, bless this food and give us humble hearts," my father said and, just in time, I saw Al's hand come away from her fork and fold itself with the other one in front of her.

"Pass the garlic bread," Teddy said and my father gave him a dirty look.

"Ladies first," he said and passed it to my mother, who took a piece and passed it to Al.

"Everything was delicious," Al said to my mother when we were clearing the table. "Absolutely delicious."

"It's a pleasure having you here, Al," my mother said. I have trained her not to say Alexandra. "A real pleasure. Come again soon."

I walked Al back to her apartment but my mother had said to get back fast and buckle down to my homework.

"You want me to come in for a sec while you turn the lights on?" I asked when we got to the door. Once in a while when I get home before anybody else I don't like to walk into the dark rooms with no one in them.

"Oh, that's all right," she said, fumbling for her key. She wears it on a chain around her neck, which causes her front to be sort of lumpy. "I always leave all the lights on when I go out."

"What time does your mother get home from her dinner engagement?" I asked.

"Usually late," she said, putting the key in the lock. "It's neat. I can do whatever I want. Sometimes I watch TV until real late and slip into bed when I hear her coming."

Her door opened and, sure enough, the hall light was on, and the one in the living room.

"It was great," she said. "It was very delicious. Tell your mother for me."

I said, "Sure. See you."

"You know something?" she said. "I can remember when I was a little tiny kid and my father used to say grace. I can remember it clear as anything. It used to make me feel like I was a pilgrim or something. You know?"

I said, "Sure," and then she clicked the lock and I went home.

Chapter Seven

"Mom," I said, "don't you think it's about time you had Al's mother over? You know, for a drink or a cup of tea?"

My mother said, "I suppose so."

"Well," I said, "you're always telling me to be friendly and nice to new kids who come to school. Some day I may be a new kid myself and in bad need of a friend. Isn't that what you say?"

"Yes," she said, "you're right. It's just that with her work and my family there isn't much opportunity."

"You're making excuses," I said. It was what she always says to me when I try to get out of something, like a D in a French test.

"Yes," she said, "I'm making excuses."

"How come you don't like Al's mother? She is really very nice."

"How can I like or not like her when I don't know her?"

"That's just it," I said. "You are judging on first impressions and appearances."

"You certainly have total recall when it suits you," my mother said, shaking her head. "I hear my words coming back at me as if there were a tape recorder in the house."

"Mom, I think it would be nice. I know Al would like it if you would ask her mother over. It would be a nice gesture."

My mother went to the chest in the dining ell where she keeps her linen napkins and tablecloths and her box of good stationery.

"For Pete's sakes," I said, "just give her a call. You don't have to bother to write a note. She only lives in 14-C."

"If you don't mind, I'll do it my way." My mother has had this box of stationery as long as I can remember. She uses it to answer engraved wedding invitations and things like that. The paper has a thin line of blue around the edges and her initials all curlicued at the top in the same blue. My father calls it her putting-on-the-dog stationery.

Finally she licked the envelope and said, "Would

you mind just putting this in their box? I don't think a stamp is necessary."

"When did you ask her for?" I said.

"Next Sunday. I asked her and Al to come for tea."

"Do you think you could get rid of Teddy for the afternoon?"

"Outside of tying him to his bed, I don't see how," she said.

"And Daddy. Is he going to be here?" I'm not sure Al's mother would appreciate my father. I think he's funny and Al thinks he's a riot, but you never know.

"Now just stop it," my mother said. "We can't exterminate all male members of the family just to keep Al's mother happy. Don't make me sorry that I asked her."

She was right. I ran out and put the invitation in their box fast.

"My mother is inviting your mother to our house," I said to Al the next day.

"What for?"

"For tea, dope. On Sunday. You're invited too."

"I don't know," Al said. "I hope she doesn't have a previous engagement."

Al's mother sent back a note on stationery that was even more putting-on-the-dog than my mother's. It was cream-colored and about a half inch thick and had her initials in black.

"One-upmanship," my father said.

She would be delighted to come on Sunday at four. She and Alexandra would be delighted. It was so kind of my mother to ask them.

My mother started polishing silver and ironing napkins. "I wonder if I'll have time to take the curtains down and wash them," she said.

"This thing is geting out of hand," my father said when she started waxing the floors and made him sit all scrunched up in one corner of the room.

"Don't you think you should get a haircut?" my mother said, squinting at him.

"That does it." He put on his old Army jacket my mother has been trying to get rid of for years. "When the coast is clear, put a candle in the window," he said.

"Oh, dear," my mother said. "I wish I'd never got into this."

Chapter Eight

"My mother says maybe you can sleep over Friday night," Al said on our way to school. She had on her navy-blue coat that her mother bought on sale. It was a very good buy, Al said It is only a little too big. She is still growing.

"Is it for supper?" I asked.

"I'll check."

We got to school before anyone else. Even Mr. Keogh. He is usually sitting at his desk, marking papers or something, by the time we get there.

Al went behind the desk. "All right, class," she said, tugging at her ear. She really did sound like Mr. Keogh. "Let's just cut out the horsing around and get down to business. We have a lot to cover today. Yes, Herman? No, you may not go to the boy's room. It is much too early to go to the boy's room."

I was in stitches. Herman is always waving his hand to go to the boy's room. I know it isn't nice to make fun of people, but sometimes I can't help it. I think it is all right if the people you make fun of don't find out.

"And Isabel, stop making goo-goo eyes at Thomas. We do not allow our students to make goo-goo eyes at each other. It is strictly out of order. Out of order, indeed."

I was laughing so hard I was practically on the floor.

"Very good, Alexandra, very good indeed. If you were as good a student as you are a thespian, you would get straight A's."

Mr. Keogh was standing at the door. He looks very young with his hat on. It is only when he takes it off that he looks old.

It was very embarrassing to be caught in the middle of something like that. I was sorry that we had got to school early. I will not do it again.

Al was very quiet the rest of the day. Even at lunch time, when we met in our usual place, she wasn't hungry.

"He called me 'Alexandra,'" she said, breaking up little pieces of her sandwich and making balls out of them. "I must have hurt his feelings and now he doesn't like me. He's mad." She was talking about Mr. Keogh.

"He'll get over it," I said. I wondered if Al would remember about asking me to sleep over on Friday. I wanted to go and I did not want to go. Al's mother makes me nervous. She is always friendly, but she makes me nervous anyway. The last time I was there she had on pajamas with feathers on them. They were hostess pajamas, Al said. My mother doesn't wear hostess pajamas. With or without feathers.

Everything turned out all right. Al came to our apartment just before supper. She rang her special ring —two, then one, then two.

"You can come for supper Friday," she said, smiling. She does not smile often and I keep telling her she should because she has nice teeth. They are very white and even. Mine are a little on the yellow side.

"Should I bring my sleeping bag?" I asked. Practically all the times I go to friends' houses I bring my sleeping bag, on account of most of the kids I know don't have extra beds.

"We have a cot," she said, "that we use when we have guests."

In all the time I had known Al, I had never slept over. This was what my mother called An Occasion.

I brought my new nightgown and even a bathrobe

and slippers, which is silly, but my mother insisted. I knew I wouldn't use the bathrobe and slippers, but my mother was firm, very firm.

Al's mother was taking a tub when I arrived. I could smell the oil and bath salts and gunk she puts in her tub. It must clog up the drains something awful.

Al's mother had a dinner engagement. She came out wearing a black dress and said, "How are you, dear?" I have a theory that when mothers call you 'dear' it is because they can't remember your name. "I'm so glad Alexandra has such a nice little friend to keep her company."

She started to kiss Al good night but Al stuck out her hand and said, "Shake, Mom. See you." Then Al's mother left.

We had a blast. We stayed up until midnight watching television. Then we had a snack, cocoa and potato chips. Finally, when we turned the lights out, Al said, "Mr. Keogh called me 'Al' again this morning." Her voice sounded happy. "And I got a post card from my father. It was from Miami, Florida, and it said 'Swimming every day. Hope to see you soon.' "

"Good," I said. I was very sleepy. "That's great. Go to sleep."

Chapter Nine

First thing when we woke up, we checked to see if it had snowed during the night. Fortunately, it hadn't, so we decided to go down to Mr. Richards's place early. Not too early, on account of it was Saturday and he likes his shut-eye. That's what he calls it, not me.

"Well, ladies," he said, "you look a little the worse for wear."

"I slept over at Al's," I said. "We didn't get to sleep until late."

Mr. Richards winked. "When you girls get together there's no stopping you. I hope you're all set for our shop lesson this morning. I found a nail or two, a hammer, and I got me some boards out. So how about a piece of bread and butter before we start?"

He fixed us each a thick slice and poured a pile of sugar on top. We hadn't had much breakfast at Al's, on account of there was nothing in the refrigerator but yoghurt. Strawberry yoghurt.

"No, thank you," I had said when Al offered me some. "I'm not up to it today."

"It's not bad," she had said, putting it back. I noticed she didn't eat any either.

Anyway, we had two or three more pieces of bread and then a couple of cups of tea. Al put three lumps in hers and I put four. Mr. Richards didn't say boo. He put five in his.

He is a very satisfactory host. I would rather have breakfast at his house than anywhere else. Except maybe at home on Sunday. My father always makes waffles on Sunday and they are very good. He calls them superb, but I think that's stretching it a little.

Finally, we got down to business. Mr. Richards had set up a piece of plywood as a table for us to work on. He showed us how to nail the shelves in place and hammer in the nails without banging our fingers.

"It's a cinch," Al said. "I think when I get it finished I will send it to my father."

We worked along for a while and pretty soon my stomach was making noises you could hear practically a mile away. It was very embarrassing.

"Must be lunch time," Mr. Richards said. "Time for

a break. Got some soup on the stove. Care to stay and take potluck?"

Al and I had two bowlfuls each. Some time I will tell her about how he makes the soup.

"Do you like to cook?" Al asked him.

Mr. Richards shrugged his shoulders. "Now and then," he said. "You ladies know how to make a white sauce?"

We said no.

"You got to know how to make a white sauce, you want to cook. Very handy thing to know. Would you believe that when I got married my wife didn't know how to boil water even? I had to show her."

"I didn't know you were ever married," I said. I wish I had known before Al did. I don't know why but I do.

"I was just a shaver," he said. "She wasn't much older'n you two. Pretty as a picture too. But it wasn't a good thing. No, it wasn't a good thing. We was too young. She took our baby daughter and went back to her mama and papa. Too many diapers, too much work, not enough fun, not enough money. Like I say, she didn't know how to cook. Didn't want to learn. It's a bad thing to get tied down too young. Remember that, ladies."

"Mr. Richards, whatever happened to your baby daughter?" Al asked.

"Well," he said, "she's not a baby any more. She has two, three babies of her own. Must be one of 'em about your age. I sent 'em a box of candy last Christmas, I think it was. I don't know if they got it, come to think. I never did hear if they got it."

We all sat quiet for a minute.

"I'll show you how to make a white sauce," he said. "First, you melt your butter, then stir in your flour slow like, then add milk, stirring all the time. Don't stop stirring or she'll lump up on you. Very handy thing to know."

"What do you do with it when you're finished?" Al asked.

"Creamed potatoes," he said. "Creamed tuna fish. Creamed eggs."

We looked at him.

"Mr. Richards," Al said, "what I would really like to know is how to skate like you do. Skate on the floor with rags. Would you teach me how to do that?"

"Well now," he said, getting some rags out from under the sink, "that's a puzzler. I been doing it for so long I can't recollect when I started. I'll tell you one thing, though. It's not as easy as it looks."

Al took first turn and she wasn't too good.

"Glide, glide, that does it," Mr. Richards hollered.

Al gave up after a couple of falls. I went next. I wasn't much better.

"Show us again," I said. "It looks so easy when you do it."

"Young folks ain't changed a bit," Mr. Richards said, tying the rags around his sneakers. "Think they can do anything they try first time around. I told you it wasn't as easy as it looks." And he skated smoothly around the edges of his shining linoleum, smiling a big smile.

Chapter Ten

After church on Sunday my mother started buttering slices of bread and wrapping them in wet towels and waxed paper. They were so thin you could practically see through them.

Teddy came into the kitchen. For once his nose wasn't running, but he had his mouth hanging open in a way I hate. He looks like a moron when he does it.

"Mom," I said, "I thought you promised." I looked at him hard. "You have anything to do this afternoon?" I asked. "A science project over at your friend's house, or how about the movies?"

"The movie is one of those movies for mature audiences only," Teddy said with a smirk. When Teddy smirks I would like to slap his face.

"Dad's taking me to the hockey game," he said. "Boy, what a relief it'll be to get out of this house. What a lot of baloney a tea party is anyway. How come you're getting so fancy just for old Al and her mother?"

"Good question." My father came into the kitchen. "Unanswerable, but good. What have we here?"

My mother took a blue box out of the refrigerator.

"Swiss Chalet!" Teddy howled.

The Swiss Chalet is a very expensive bakery where my mother goes only when my grandmother—my father's mother—is coming to visit, which she does only about once a year. My grandmother, who is little and round and going bald like my father, has a terrific sweet tooth.

"Let's have a look," my father said.

My mother opened the box like it was full of eggs or a time bomb or something. Inside were all kinds of cookies and cakes decorated with whipped cream and shaved chocolate. "You can have one when you get back if they're any left," she said.

They both looked at her and Teddy's mouth hung open wider than ever. "I'm hungry," he whined.

"Please," my mother said. "Go get a hot dog at the game. Please." She pushed them gently toward the door.

When we heard the elevator door slam, we each breathed a sigh of relief.

My mother went into her room to get dressed.

"Mom," I said, "will you wear a little more lipstick than usual? And some of that rouge you have. And don't forget to hold in your stomach."

"Same to you," my mother said. But when she came out she looked very pretty.

"You look pretty," I said. "Your hair looks nice."

"I feel as if I was trying out for Mrs. America," she said.

"You'd win," I said.

The doorbell rang at three minutes after four. My mother smoothed her skirt and said, "Would you answer it please?"

Al's mother said, "Hello, dear, how are you?" and my mother said, "Good afternoon, won't you come in?"

We sort of stood there for a minute.

"What a sweet place," Al's mother said.

"Sit down, won't you?" my mother said.

Al smelled of tooth paste. She even had some around her mouth. "You've got tooth paste on your mouth," I said. She wiped her face on her sleeve.

"You want me to get the tea now, Mom?" I asked.

"Please," she said, then turned to Al's mother. "Unless you'd rather have some sherry? Or a drink of some sort?"

"To me," Al's mother said, "afternoon tea is one

of the few civilized customs left. It revives me." "How enchanting!" she said as I brought out the tray. My mother's silver teapot shone and, the way I'd fixed it, the bread and butter looked like a giant pin wheel.

"Will you have lemon or cream?" my mother asked as she passed the cakes.

"How delicious and how fattening!" Al's mother cried. "I hate to think of how many calories there are in each of these." She took one and put it on a plate. She only ate half.

"Would you girls get some hot water?" my mother asked. We went to the kitchen and ate a few cookies and listened.

"I want to thank you for being so kind to Alexandra," Al's mother said. "I have to be away from home so much of the time, it's a comfort to me to know she can call on you if she should need to."

"We like Al," my mother said. "She is a very nice child. We all like her."

"Of course," Al's mother went on, "she is very self-sufficient. She has been on her own a good deal and I think that tends to make them self-sufficient, don't you?"

"I suppose so," my mother said. "Will you have another cup of tea?"

"Thank you. I will. It was so kind of you to ask us," Al's mother said. "I've been wanting to get to know you better ever since we moved in, but what with my job, I don't get nearly enough chance to see people."

"We are so glad you could come."

They talked about different places Al and her mother had lived and about the store where Al's mother works.

Then Al's mother looked at her watch.

"Where has the time gone?" she asked. "I had no idea it was so late. I'm afraid we must run, but before we do, I want to thank you again for all your kindness to Alexandra. It has meant a great deal to her, I know, to be a part of your family fun. I try, but I cannot make up for not being a real family. Just the two of us is hard, sometimes. It is difficult, doing it alone."

"I can well imagine," my mother said. "It is often difficult even with the help of a man."

The front door opened and my father and Teddy came in.

"May I present my husband?" my mother said.

My father took Al's mother's hand, and instead of shaking it, he sort of bowed. He bowed low over her hand. He didn't kiss it, but he looked like he might.

Al dug her elbow into my ribs. Teddy's mouth hung open and Al's mother said, "How delightful to meet you. Al's told me so much about you."

My father smiled. "I wish I could have gotten home sooner," he said.

"It's been such fun," Al's mother said, and they left.

My mother started to carry the tray out. "Charm was certainly oozing from every pore," she said.

Teddy crammed a whole mouthful of bread and cookies into his mouth, so for once, it was closed.

"Was it all right?" my mother asked.

"It was great," I said. "Just great. I think they liked it. Thanks, Mom. Al's mother is really very nice, don't you think?"

"Very nice," she said. "Do you think those fingernails were real?"

My father went over to my mother and bent over her hand, nibbling his way up her arm like he was eating an ear of corn.

"Not on your tintype," he said.

Chapter Eleven

"I have been invited to Al's for supper," I told my mother. "Her mother is out for dinner and she gave Al money to get a pizza. Please."

"Let her come here instead," my mother said, darning a hole in my father's sock. Darning always makes her cross.

"She says she's been here too much and that her mother wants to repay our hospitality."

"It's a school night." She sighed and put down the darning. I have noticed that she will use almost any excuse to put down darning.

"We'll do our homework together and we promise not to watch television," I said.

"You can go if you'll be home by eight-thirty," she said.

"You're the mother of my dreams," I told her.

I put my books in a pile and went to Al's. She had all the lights in the entire apartment on. It made the house cosier, she said.

We went down to the corner to Angelo's and ordered a sausage-and-pepper pizza. To go. I wanted to stay there and eat it and watch Angelo throw the dough in the air and catch it and make the different kinds that people ordered, but Al said, "Let's take it home."

It was still warm when we got it back, on account of we ran. We each had a Coke because, though I would rather have milk, all they have is skimmed milk, which is pale gray, and I don't find it too appetizing.

"Your mother," I said when we were eating, "where does she go when she goes out all the time?"

"She goes dancing, mostly," Al said. "She is a very good dancer. Or else they go to a play or the movies or something."

"Does she, you know, does she go steady? With any one person, I mean."

Al got a little red. "You don't go steady when you are my mother's age," she said. "She has to have masculine companionship. She has a very demanding job and a lot of women telling her what to do, and she likes masculine companionship."

"Do you think she'll ever get married again?" I asked, helping myself to another piece of pizza.

"I doubt it." Al hit the bottom of the Coke bottle with her straw and gave a big slurp.

"Who's she out with tonight?" I asked.

"The one I told you about. The one who wanted to take me to the circus. Can you imagine!" Al rolled her eyes. "Me, at the circus!"

"What's the matter with that?" I asked.

"At my age, go to the circus? Are you crazy? I outgrew it years ago. My father wouldn't dream of any dumb thing like that. He'd take me out to a snazzy place for dinner and then maybe to an art film."

"What's an art film?" I asked.

"Where they speak in a foreign language and have little lines underneath that tell you in English what they're saying."

"You like art films?" I asked.

"Not really." She shrugged. "Anyway, this one's name is Mr. Herbert Smith and he said, 'Call me Herb,' if you can feature such a thing. At least he didn't say 'Call me Uncle Herb.' That's the living end when they want you to call them 'Uncle' and they're not your uncle. I can't stand that. Anyway, he's trying to buy me." She made her eyes big and round like an owl's.

"What do you mean, trying to buy you?" I asked. "You're no bargain." I looked at her.

"Like, he brings me things. He brought me a pair of slippers tonight. A pair of fuzzy slippers like a kid's. He buys me something almost every time he comes to take my mother out. He thinks it makes me like him. And I want to tell you he is very much mistaken. Very much mistaken indeed." Al paced back and forth with her hands behind her back.

"Were they the right size?" I asked.

She said, "What?"

"The slippers. Were they the right size?"

She snorted. "I didn't try them on. I just said 'Thank you' and put them back in the box."

"Your father buys you things and you don't think he's trying to get you to like him, do you?"

"That's different. He's my father."

My father hardly ever buys me things. He sends me a Valentine every year that he picks out, but outside of that, my mother does the buying.

"Does your mother like Herb better'n any of the others she goes out with?" I asked.

Al hunched her shoulders. "I don't know. All I

know is, when he's coming I have to comb my hair and put on a clean blouse and I have to smile until my face feels like it's cracking. Then he tells me about how I remind him of his niece's little girl and it turns out she's about six and her teeth stick out and she has her own horse. If there's anything I hate, it's a kid who has her own horse. Are they ever stuck-up. They are such snobs when they own their own horse."

"Let's have some pie for dessert," Al said suddenly. She switches subjects very fast. It is interesting. You never get time to be bored.

"We have coconut cream," she said from inside the freezer compartment.

I felt like I had a giant ball of pizza and Coke inside me. "No, thanks," I said. What I didn't need was to add a little coconut cream.

"I have to write my autobiography for English," Al said. "I have to make it interesting and informative. I also need a picture of myself when I was little. Boy, was I ever a funny-looking kid." She started to laugh.

"So was I," I said. "My mother said she felt better when she saw her babies were funny-looking. She said the funnier-looking they are when they're born, the better they turn out in the long run."

"No kidding?" Al went and looked at herself in the

mirror. "Is that right? If it is, I should be a winner."

We got down to our homework but it was sort of hard because Al was in a real chatty mood.

"Imagine if we were sisters," she said. "And we lived in the same house and slept in the same room and did our homework together every night. I wonder if we'd fight. Do you think we would?"

"Yes," I said.

"Have you ever wanted a sister?" Al asked.

"I'd trade Teddy in on a sister, if that's what you mean," I said.

"He's better'n nothing," Al said. Then she started doing her math. When she does her math she breathes hard, thumps around, and stares at the ceiling and sighs. Finally I said, "Would you please shut up? I can't think."

It was time for me to go. "I've got to be back by eight-thirty or my mother will never let me come again on a school night."

"I'll walk you down the hall," she said.

"You don't have to do that," I said.

"I know I don't," she said. She turned on the television.

"What'd you do that for?" I said as we went out the door.

"It's nice to come back and hear voices," she said. "It's sort of like coming in to a party or a whole bunch of people. You know?"

"Sure," I said. "Thanks for the pizza."

Chapter Twelve

Al has always been a little on the fat side, but lately I've noticed she is starting to bulge. I don't mean she is starting to get a figure. I mean she bulges at her waist and she has a couple of chins. She's even got creases in her neck, like a baby, but on a baby it looks O.K.

"What's up?" I finally asked her. "You pack away candy bars and junk like there was no tomorrow. Where do you get all the dough? You inherit a million dollars or something?"

"I have more money than I know what to do with," Al said, pulling back the wrapper from her latest purchase. "My mother gives me an allowance, right? Which I either put in the bank, where it stagnates, or else I blow it. On myself. My father sends me checks. He sent me ten dollars last week. For nothing. Not a birthday, not anything. So you see."

Al pushed her glasses back up on her nose. They slide down lots of times.

"Want me to treat you?"

I was tempted, to be sure. My mother and father would give you the shirt off their back, but they would just as soon not give you any extra money, on account of they do not have any. That and they think their kids ought to work for what they get. My father says this is an old-fashioned idea but he is an old-fashioned man.

I am almost always broke. I am used to it by now.

"No, thanks," I said. "My mother got the dentist bill last week and she is really cracking down. She says she is going to make Teddy and me pay our own bills if we don't stop eating candy and chewing gum."

"If I know your mother," Al said, "when she says it, she will do it. She is a tough cookie, your mother. No offense. I mean it in a nice way. I like your mother. She is a good egg."

We walked down the hall to our lockers.

"My mother took me to the doctor so he could put me on a diet," Al said. "She says I am getting so gross she can hardly stand it. She gets very upset when people get fat. She says there is absolutely no excuse for it. Being in Better Dresses, as she is, she sees quite a lot of fat women who would give their eyeteeth to get into a size ten. She says if you are fat you might as well forget about looking good in clothes. She thinks a lot about clothes," Al said, "being in the business and all."

As we went down the front steps Martha Moseley was standing there at the bottom, with a bunch of kids all around. Martha is a pain. Her sister is a cheerleader at the high school and Martha is always jumping around and showing off, twirling a baton and practicing cheerleading.

"Tub a butter, tub a lard, hit 'em again and hit 'em hard," Martha yelled. I didn't notice the first time because, as I say, she is always hollering about something. But when I saw the kids snickering behind their hands, I listened.

"Tub a butter, tub a lard, hit 'em again and hit 'em hard," Martha yelled once more. I looked at Al. Her face was practically the color of a beet, which is one vegetable I really hate.

"I think I will sock her in the nose," I said. "She is really a brat. Ever since the first grade she has been a brat and people get more so as they get older, my mother says."

Al said, "I have gained five pounds in the last two weeks."

"I thought you said the doctor put you on a diet," I said.

"He did. He put me on a rigid diet."

I waited.

"I am supposed to eat yoghurt and cottage cheese and lean meat and vegetables without butter. And grapefruit. I eat grapefruit until it comes out my ears. Then I'm so hungry I sneak a couple of peanut-butter sandwiches and a banana or two."

Al stopped walking suddenly.

"Tell me something. Do you think how a person looks is the most important thing about the person? How about what they're like inside. For instance, take Mr. Richards. He is a lovely man, the best. He looks a little old and beat-up and maybe not like an actor or anything, but inside he is a good man. If he was good-looking on the outside and mean and stingy on the inside, that would be terrible. Right?"

"Yes," I said. "That is true. But people do sort of judge you by how you look, at least until they really get to know you, and it is sort of nice to look good. You know, to feel you look as good as you can. Like the way you look when your hair isn't braided and you have that blue sweater on."

"Hah!" Al said. "That blue sweater wouldn't button

around me in a million years. As a matter of fact, I can hardly fit into any of my clothes. *She* is having a fit, as you can well imagine. She says she will not buy me anything new until I lose some weight.

"And you know something? I don't care! I don't care a darn!" Al shouted. "If she has to buy me Chubbies, then she has to buy me Chubbies!"

"What are Chubbies?" I asked.

"They are dresses that people who are fat have to wear. They are quite disgusting-looking, and frankly, I think my mother, being in Better Dresses, would be humiliated if she had to buy me a Chubby."

She smiled at me with her mouth.

I did not know what to say.

Chapter Thirteen

"You two young ladies are getting very grown up," Mr. Richards said. "I swear, in a couple of months I won't know you. You'll grow up tall and good-looking and you'll have so many young fellas at your doorstep you won't know what to do with 'em all."

Al and I looked at each other. We have both decided that we will probably never get married and will share an apartment and have a cat or two and a dog or two and never do any wash except when we want to. We will only change the sheets when we want and we will also only eat and sleep when we want.

My father says the best of all possible worlds does not exist, but I think this would be close to it.

"We're never going to get married," Al said. Mr. Richards listened like he always does, and he skated around the floor a few times while she finished telling him about our plan.

"Well, now," he said, "I don't think that's such a hot idea. Like I say, when these young fellas start courting you two, you'll learn to pick and choose. You lose a little of that baby fat," he said, looking at Al, "and you'll be a real looker. Yes, sir, a stunner."

"And you"—he turned to me—"when you grow into your bones and learn not to stoop over but to stand up proud and tall, you might even be a model."

Secretly, I have planned all along on being a model. I have never told this to anyone except once to Al when I was sleeping over at her house. I looked at her to see if she looked guilty, if she had told him. Instead, she looked like she was about to explode.

"Baby fat!" she hollered. "I'm so gross my mother has to buy me Chubbies. Why, I bet I weigh more than you do."

Mr. Richards said, "I wouldn't put it past you," and all of a sudden we were all laughing. We laughed so long and so hard that my stomach ached, and tears were rolling down Mr. Richards's face, and Al said, over and over, "Oh, oh, oh."

"A good laugh is good for the soul," Mr. Richards said when we finally calmed down. "Now how about some carrot sticks?"

He has taken to keeping carrot sticks in ice water in his refrigerator, I have noticed. Another thing, Mr.

Richards is a very tactful man. That is, he would not say, "I am giving you carrot sticks instead of bread and butter and sugar because they are not fattening." He does not say anything that would embarrass anyone, ever. We helped ourselves and then he said, "What I was saying when I was interrupted was that you two young ladies, when you set your minds to it, are going to be beauties. You got all the makings if only you'll just put 'em all together at the right time. Yes, sir, I want to be around when the lines start to form outside your doors. Yes sirree."

This is a new idea and Al and I will have to think it over. It is not unpleasant. But I'll tell you one thing. If it turns out the way he says, I will never giggle and twitch my rear when I walk down the street, like some people I know.

"Mr. Richards, I've been thinking," Al said, helping herself to another carrot stick. "I've been thinking about your daughter and how she has children of her own. So they're your grandchildren. Right?"

"Right as rain."

"What do they look like? How many boys and how many girls?"

"I don't rightly know," he said. "I never have seen 'em. I wrote a letter or two and said I'd be pleased to see 'em, but I never got an answer. They live a long way away and I guess maybe they don't know about me. I been gone a long time and maybe their mother doesn't think I should come around. I wasn't all that much of a father to her."

Mr. Richards sat down. "Like I said, my wife wasn't much older'n you two and pretty as a picture. She wrote me that she got married again some time after she left. A big handsome fella. Made good money, I understand. I sent some money to my daughter three, four times, and after a couple times, she sent it back. Said she didn't need it, they was getting along fine. It cut me up some at the time, I remember."

Al said fiercely, "That wasn't very nice."

"It was her way. She was proud. So was I, although about what I don't know. Folks do things they're not happy to recollect, that's for sure."

He stood up and said, "Here's a trick I bet you can't do." He put a book on his head and walked around the room and the book didn't tip even a little bit.

"Can you skate around the kitchen with that on your head?" I asked and Mr. Richards said, "I believe that is beyond me." He tried anyhow and we had another fit of hysterics on account of he bounced the book off his big toe and hobbled around pretending that he had broken it.

"I have never laughed so hard in my whole entire

life," Al said after we'd said good-by and were on our way up in the elevator. "I wish Mr. Richards was our age so that he could be our friend all through our lives."

"It wouldn't be the same," I said. "It is much better that he is old. I can't feature him being a grandfather and all and never seeing his grandchildren, though. Or his daughter. It seems very strange. I mean, most fathers really think their daughters are special. They say fathers are partial to daughters. I don't know why that is. Doesn't it seem strange to you?"

"You are a conformist," Al said in a cold tone. "You think everyone should follow all the rules. They don't, I can tell you. How about if I ever get married. Just suppose I do. Then if I had babies my father would be their grandfather and he wouldn't come to see them."

"How do you know?" I said.

"Well," she said, "if he doesn't come to see me, he's certainly not going to come to see them, is he? That's logical."

She stomped off at our floor and didn't even say "See you" like she usually does.

It wasn't until I got into bed that night and thought about it that I knew I'd hurt Al's feelings. What a dumb thing to say to her, that fathers think daughters

are so great. That was terrible. Her father only sends
her postcards and money. He doesn't even come to see
her. I could kill myself for being so dumb. I will
apologize first chance I get, but I doubt if that will
make her feel any better.

Chapter Fourteen

My brother Teddy has a bad cold. He looks terrible. His eyes are all red and runny, just like his nose, and he makes the most disgusting noises.

"Play Monopoly with me?" he sort of whined.

"No," I said. "I have to do my social-studies project." I was going to do it with Al, but now I don't know. My mother had baked gingerbread just before I got home from school. It has a very good smell, better than lots of perfumes. Too bad they can't bottle the smell of gingerbread cooking. They would make a fortune.

"Boy, that's a delicious smell," I said. "Smell that gingerbread?"

The end of Teddy's nose quivered. "You know I can't smell it," he said. "I'm all stuffed up."

"Too bad," I said. "It's the best smell."

"How come Al hasn't been around lately?" Teddy whined. "She usually practically sleeps here."

"She's my best friend," I said.

"Last week she wasn't."

"Wasn't what?"

"I saw her at the movies last week with a couple of other girls. She was real palsy-walsy with them, is all I can say. I don't think you're her best friend. She may be yours, but you're not hers."

I got Teddy's shoulder in a real hold. I dug my fingers down in that little place that's just made for pinching. It hurts. I know.

"Shut your mouth," I whispered, because my mother was in the kitchen. "One more word out of you and I'll let you have it right between the eyes. Now shut up."

Two big tears squeezed out of Teddy's eyes and dribbled down his cheeks. He didn't even bother to wipe them away. He is a real mess.

I let go of his shoulder. "I will go and get you a piece of gingerbread," I said, "and I will play Monopoly with you for exactly one half hour. No more, no less. Set it up and I'll be right back."

I did not look at him but as I went out I could hear him snuffling.

"Doesn't that kid know how to blow his nose?" I said.

"People who live in glass houses," my mother said. "Be my guest." And she handed me a box of tissues.

Chapter Fifteen

"How's Al?" my mother asked. "Have you had a fight?"

"She's O.K., I guess," I said, blowing my nose. "Why do you want to know?"

"Well, I haven't seen her in a couple of days and that's sort of unusual. I just wondered if you'd had a misunderstanding or if she was sick or something."

She started shredding the cabbage for supper. "Ordinarily, you two live in each other's pockets."

"I have other friends, don't forget," I said. "You are always saying we see too much of each other. So we have decided to have other friends."

"Fine," my mother said. "But why don't you ask her over for supper tonight? Isn't she usually alone for supper? It wouldn't be much fun, I should think, to eat alone all the time."

"You may not think so, but she doesn't have anyone to tell her to go to bed, stop watching TV, do your homework, stuff like that."

"I know," my mother said. "That's what I mean."

"She is probably over at Susie's house. Or Wendy's."

My mother put lotion on her hands. She does this all the time but I have noticed that my father does not carry on the way men do in TV commercials when their wives use hand lotion, about how soft and everything their hands are. About how they're as white and pretty as before they got married. Sometimes you have to stop and think about things like that.

"Run down the hall and see if she's there, please, like a good girl. I made too much chili and I've got coleslaw and she loves coleslaw."

I went but I didn't run. I walked. Very slowly. I rang Al's bell. Just a regular ring, nothing special.

"Hi," I said.

Al said, "Hello."

"My mother wants to know if you want to come to supper tonight," I said.

Al looked like she'd have to think if she had a previous engagement. My mother does the same thing.

"I don't know," she said. "I have a lot of homework."

"My mother said to tell you we're having chili."

"Oh," said Al.

"And coleslaw," I said. "And Al, I'm sorry."

"About what?" Al said.

"About the stupid dumb thing I said the other day. About fathers thinking daughters were a big deal. I could kill myself, it was so dumb."

"That's all right," Al said. "I didn't think anything about it." She smiled. "Tell your mother that I would like to come. Very much. That is very nice of her."

"O.K.," I said. "Come at six. See you."

Chapter Sixteen

We went down to Mr. Richards's to check on our bookshelves. We had put the glue on them a couple of days ago and we wanted to see how they had turned out. They looked pretty nice and Mr. Richards said when we put a coat of shellac on them they would be all set to go.

"It is the first thing I have ever made by myself," Al said. "I think it's pretty good."

"You girls should be proud, real proud," Mr. Richards said. "I never thought you could do such a good job."

We both smiled.

"Have a shooter?" he asked.

"No, thanks," Al said. "I have been invited out to dinner and I want to save my appetite."

"Who invited you?" I said.

"Mr. Herbert Smith is who," Al said. "He invited me and my mother out to dinner. How about that?"

"Mr. Herbert Smith is a friend of Al's mother," I explained to Mr. Richards. "He takes her out."

"That so? He must be a mighty nice fella."

"There's one thing that bothers me," Al said. "I've been thinking about what I should talk about. I should have an interesting topic to talk about so we don't have big long silences and they'll be sorry they brought me along. It is the first time I have been invited out like this."

"How about air pollution?" Mr. Richards said. "It is a very good topic. Everybody is interested in air pollution. I have been reading a lot about it in the papers. The stuff you take into your lungs when you go out for a breath of air these days, you wouldn't believe. It is not safe to breathe too much, you coat your lungs with poison. Pure poison. It is very interesting. After all," he said, "we all got lungs."

"You are right," Al said.

"Just sit tight," he said, "and I will find the story I am talking about." He scuffled around through a big stack of papers and came up with a long, boring-looking story.

"You read this here," he said, giving it to Al, "and

you'll have them thinking you are a very smart young lady who knows what is going on in the world today."

"Thank you, Mr. Richards. I don't know what I'd do without you," Al said.

We said good-by and went out to the elevator.

"I think maybe my father is coming to see me," Al said on our way up.

"That's nice," I said. "When is he coming? I would like to meet him."

"I'm not exactly sure. He said he might drop in. He is at a convention in the city. Either he'll drop in or maybe he'll invite me to a hotel for dinner and maybe go to a play."

"Will your mother go too?" I asked.

"I don't know," she said. "My mother and father have a very friendly relationship, you know."

If they have a very friendly relationship, I do not see why they are divorced, but that is none of my business.

"That's nice," I said. Al never talks about her mother and father and I have always wanted to know why they got divorced.

"Excuse me," I said, "I know it is none of my business, but I would like to know why your mother and father got a divorce."

Al said, "My father is a perfectionist. My mother says no woman can stand being married to a perfectionist."

"Oh," I said.

I don't think either my mother or my father is a perfectionist.

I am glad.

Chapter Seventeen

It was snowing when I woke up the next morning.
My brother Teddy was over his cold and was acting
like an idiot, leaping around and throwing his oatmeal
in the dog's dish so he could get outside faster.

The dog does not like oatmeal, so he left it.

I like everything but liver. The dog loves it. His
nose quivers when my mother cooks liver. She would
not like it if she knew the dog got mine. She would
have a fit, in fact. At those prices.

Anyway, my mother came in, and when she saw the
oatmeal in the dog's dish, she started hollering at
Teddy about wasting food.

He put his hand in front of his mouth and started
imitating her. He always gets spoiled when he has a
head cold. He is getting extremely fresh for a nine
year old. I would not dare to imitate my mother in
front of her. I would at least wait until she left the

room. Teddy says this is sneaky. He is my mother's favorite. Most girls I know say their brother is their mother's favorite. It is sort of an unwritten law.

I will admit, though, that the last time he came to the table and made a face and said, "What? Pork chops again!" she sent him to his room and he didn't get any supper at all.

She said she would do it and she did. My mother is very consistent. It is one of the best things and one of the worst things about her.

It was a pretty snow, with big, wet flakes.

"This won't last," my father said. He considers himself an authority on snow and whether or not it will last.

"I hope not, sort of," I said. "We are just about to finish our bookshelves. We have to put a coat of shellac on them and then they are set. If it's a big snow, Mr. Richards will have to shovel walks and we will not be able to get much done."

"It's a pity his job cuts into your woodworking," my mother said. She still does not like me to go down there all the time, but when she found out me and Al were doing something useful she didn't mind so much. She even said, "I suppose you'd like me to invite Mr. Richards for tea too."

I got hysterical thinking about Mr. Richards coming

into our apartment and sitting down and saying he'd like a shooter of tea. I laughed so hard I couldn't breathe and she had to thump me on the back.

"Why don't you kids give him a hand after school?" my father said. "That old geezer shouldn't be shoveling, especially a heavy, wet snow like this. He must be getting on for seventy."

"Seventy's not so old," I said. "Gosh, they're plenty of kings and presidents and actors and all kinds of people who are seventy."

"True," my father said, "but they're not necessarily out shoveling snow."

He has a point.

I met Al in the hall.

"How was it?" I said. "Did you have a good time with Mr. Smith?"

"We went to a fantastic place," she said. "It had rugs on the floor so thick I went in up to my ankles. And I had crepes suzette for dessert—you know, those pancakes they set on fire. It was pretty cool."

"How did the air pollution go?" I said.

"Well, I told them about it and what you breathed when you went out and what your lungs looked like and all. They were pretty interested but my mother changed the subject and we talked about comic strips.

Mr. Smith likes "Peanuts" and a whole mess of others and we got along pretty well. He's not such a bad egg."

"That's good," I said. "I'm glad you like him better."

It snowed all the way to school.

"If this keeps up," I said, "I think it would be good if we helped Mr. Richards shovel. So he won't have a heart attack or something. He must be getting on for seventy."

"Good idea," she said. She put out her tongue and caught some snow on it. "It tastes like chocolate," she said.

I put out my tongue and it didn't taste like anything to me except snow. "Mine tastes like vanilla," I said.

I have learned to go along with the gag, as Al says.

Chapter Eighteen

"How do you like my new tie?" Mr. Keogh wanted to know.

"Well," I said, "it is different." It was blue and red and yellow in a sort of squiggly pattern. It would be good for Saturdays.

"I'll tell you frankly, Mr. Keogh," Al said, "it doesn't do too much for you. If you know what I mean."

Mr. Keogh looked down at his tie. "Indeed I do know, Al. Indeed I do. And I'm a man who needs all the help he can get."

He winked at us and we had a good laugh. We are all friends.

"Mr. Keogh," I said, "I thought you might be interested to know that Al and I are practically finished making bookshelves. At home, I mean. Mr. Richards, who is our assistant superintendent, is teaching us on Saturday mornings. We are coming along pretty good."

"That's fine. I'm glad to hear it. How are you coming along on your social-studies project? Just as good?"

Al and I are doing a project on different countries for social studies.

"Mr. Keogh, I have written to all the embassies and information bureaus of all the places I want to find out more about, and I have probably got more stuff in the mail than any other kid in our class," I said.

"How'd you manage that?" Mr. Keogh asked.

"Well," I said, "my father tipped me off. He told me if I wrote for information and just signed 'Miss' they would think I was only some little upstart kid. Whereas, if I signed my letter 'Mrs.' or put 'Mrs.' on the back of the envelope, they would think maybe I would take a trip to their country with all my children and my husband and they would make a lot of money from me. So I put 'Mrs.' on the back of the envelope and they sent me everything in sight."

"Excellent," Mr. Keogh said. "Tell your father I think he is a very clever man. The only thing is—and he straightened his new tie—"the mailman must be a little perplexed. When he has all this mail addressed to 'Mrs.' and he gets a load of you, he must wonder what monkey business is going on."

"Oh," I said, "we don't see our mailman all that much. He only really comes around at Christmas time. He starts bringing this big load of mail just about a week or so before Christmas. His feet hurt something terrible but he still brings this mail right to our door instead of dropping it in the box."

"Hm," Mr. Keogh said, "we must share the same mailman."

Chapter Nineteen

By the time we got out of school the snow had stopped.

My father was right.

"I wonder if Mr. Richards will have to shovel any of this," Al said. "I should think those lazy old tenants could do a little work themselves. Mr. Richards is much too fine a man to be at their beck and call. You know something?"

Al stuck her hands on her hips and stopped in the middle of the sidewalk.

"No. What?" I said.

"Mr. Richards is a prince. He is the nicest man I know. Outside of Mr. Keogh."

"How about my father?" I asked. "I thought you liked my father a lot."

Al got red. "Yes," she said, "I do. He is great. And for that matter, how about my father?" She sounded like Teddy does when he is looking for a fight, which is a lot of the time.

"I don't know your father," I said. "But from his picture I would say he would be nice, very nice. I like his eyebrows."

Al turned and started walking again. "Don't forget," she said, "Just don't forget that Mr. Keogh and your father have perfectly good wives and families."

I nodded. "That is true." Mr. Keogh's wife has a little baby boy. I have seen pictures of him and if he had a bow tie on he'd look just like Mr. Keogh.

Al walked very fast. I had a hard time keeping up.

"Mr. Richards has no one. He is all alone. That is very important."

By this time we were practically running.

"He doesn't seem to mind," I said finally, when I could get my breath. "He never seems to be lonely."

Sometimes I think that Al does not remember that I have known Mr. Richards a lot longer than she has. I have never said this to her but I think it. She acts kind of uppity about Mr. Richards sometimes, like she discovered him or something.

"That's all you know." Al narrowed her eyes so they were little slits, like Mr. Richards's. "That's all you know."

When we got out at our floor I asked Al if she wanted to come in for a snack. Practically every day we go to my house for a snack on account of Al's mother doesn't believe in snacks.

"No," she said. "Thanks, but I am cutting down on snacks. That and I want to see if there's a letter or anything from my father. I am sort of expecting to hear from him today."

"Did you check the mail?" I asked.

"I forgot," Al said. "I will drop off my books and go back and check."

"O.K." I said. "I think my mother made brownies, if you change your mind." I could smell them. As a matter of fact, I could almost see the smell coming out from under the door. The way it does in the funny papers. Big waves of smell. It is a nice thing to come home to.

"How was your day?" my mother asked. One thing about my mother, she is usually glad to see me. Not always, but usually.

"Pretty good," I said. "Can I have a brownie?"

"One," she said. "Did I hear you talking to Al?"

"She went back to check the mail. She expects to hear from her father today. He is coming to see her soon."

"That's nice," she said.

I heard the elevator stop and I went to the door.

"Did you get a letter?" I asked.

"No," she said.

"Maybe that means he is on a plane right now and will just call you up," I said. "He's probably just about over our heads right now," I said, and sure enough, we could hear an airplane going over very low, getting ready to land. We live pretty near the airport and get so used to the noise we don't even think about it.

"Maybe," she said.

"How about a brownie?" I asked. "My mother just made them."

"No offense," Al said, "but I am not in the mood right now. And I am on a diet."

She fished around for her front-door key. "I am going to wash my face and brush my teeth and fix my hair," she said.

"Oh," I said, "that way you will be all ready for when your father calls."

"No," she said, "I thought it might be fun if we went to see Mr. Richards."

"Oh, all right," I said. We never get dolled up for him, I felt like saying. He is not the kind of person who expects people to get dolled up. I was about to say this to Al when she said, "I'll stop by for you when I'm ready," and went into her apartment.

"Did Al hear from her father?" my mother asked.

"Not today," I said.

Mr. Richards was not there when we arrived, so we sat down to wait. He came in about five minutes later.

"Had to put ashes on that ice out by them garbage pails," he said. "Well, ladies, tell me about yourselves. How was your dinner date?" he said to Al. "You give 'em the air pollution stuff?"

"They thought it was great," she said. "We had a nice time. I had crepes suzette. You know what they are?"

"You bet," Mr. Richards said. "Them little pancakes you light up. I never had 'em myself but I used to work in a classy restaurant where they had 'em. Always wanted to try 'em for myself."

We looked at each other.

"Why not?" Al said.

"Well"—he got out a frying pan—"I'll give it a whirl, but I don't know. I'm more of a flapjack man myself."

We watched while he threw some flour, eggs, milk, and sugar into a bowl and sizzled some butter in the pan. When he had a stack of about six cakes he put two on each plate.

"How do you get it to flame up?" Al said.

"I reckon brandy," Mr. Richards said. "I keep a bottle of brandy for toothache. I'll pour a mite on and set a match to 'em and we'll see what we get."

He put a tiny bit of brandy on top of each cake and lit them. They flamed up pretty well.

Mr. Richards took the first bite.

"I'll take mine with maple syrup any day," he said. "What say, ladies? You agree?"

Al said, "Delicious," but she couldn't help making a face and we wound up throwing the rest in the garbage.

"Stick to flapjacks and you can't go wrong," Mr. Richards said. I agree.

Chapter Twenty

"I'm going shopping after school," Al said. "You want to come?" We always get out early Friday afternoon, so I told her, "Sure. What are you going shopping for?"

"I have decided to buy myself a sweater with the money I got from my father. I figure ten dollars ought to be about right."

"I thought your mother always bought your clothes at her employee discount," I said. "Will she think it is all right for you to go to some place else and pay full price?"

"It is my money," Al said. "I have decided to take the bull by the horns and buy myself something nice to wear. Instead of buying myself junk. Food junk. You know."

She looked at me like she was expecting me to argue

with her. I thought the whole idea was great. Beautiful. I told her so.

"Beautiful," I said. "I will help you pick it out. What color do you want?"

"I think I will have pink. Pink is a good color. My mother says elderly women buy pink so the reflection will make them look young. They even have pink lamp shades in restaurants so that the ladies will look young."

"But you are not elderly," I said.

"So what?" Al shrugged. "Some days I feel awful old."

She tossed a pigtail over her shoulder. "Let's go," she said.

"One thing I know," I said as we went downtown, "one thing that would make you look better is if you stopped wearing those pigtails. Comb your hair out and it looks great. It kind of shines and it's real pretty."

"Holy Toledo," Al said, "you'd think I was trying out for Miss Teen Queen of America," but she looked pleased and her cheeks got pink even though she had on a white blouse.

We went to the sweater department of the store, which was not the one where Al's mother worked.

"Yes?" The lady gave us the fishy eye. They must

train salesladies to give the fishy eye. She acted like we had a large paper sack under each arm and were preparing to stuff them full of sweaters and run for the nearest exit.

"I want a pink sweater," Al said.

"What size?"

Al said, "I don't know. I have never bought a sweater for myself before."

The saleslady stood back and narrowed her eyes. "I would say a thirty-six," she said and reached into a glass case and came out with a couple of pink sweaters.

Al said, "I will take this one."

"Don't you want to try it on?"

"I'm going to wear it," Al said. "That is, if I can afford it. How much is it?"

"With tax, that comes to nine dollars and forty-five cents," the lady said. "But you'd better slip it on and see if it fits. There's a dressing room back here."

Al slipped it on and it fit fine, which was a good thing because I think she would have worn it even if it hadn't fit.

"It looks very nice," I said, because it was what she wanted to hear and also because it was true. "That color is good on you." This is what my mother always says.

All the way home Al kept running her hand over the sleeve of the sweater.

"I don't think I've ever had a pink sweater before. It's the first thing I've really bought for myself. To wear, that is. It is a good feeling to buy something for yourself to wear. You know? I will write my father and thank him for the check and tell him what I did with it. I think he would like that. Maybe I will have a picture of myself taken wearing the sweater and send it to him. Do you think that would be good?"

"That's a great idea," I said. "Then he can show it to all his friends and say, 'This is my daughter.' He would probably like that a lot."

"You know something?" Al said. "I don't think he's ever really going to come to see me. I just decided that now. I think he thinks he will, but he'll never make it. Sort of like Mr. Richards never getting to see his daughter and his grandchildren. He wanted to, but he never did."

"Oh, no," I said. "He'll come when he isn't too busy. Men get awfully busy. He'll come when he isn't on a trip."

"Do you really believe that?" Al asked me.

"He thinks about you," I said. "He sends you money and most kids' fathers don't even give them a quarter without an argument."

"That is true," Al said. "But I feel sorry for him. I am the only daughter he's got and he'll never really know me. Just like Mr. Richards will never know his daughter. And she's the only one he's got. That is really kind of sad, don't you think?"

"Yes," I said. "I agree. It is sad."

"I'll write him tonight," she said. "I'll tell him exactly how much it cost, tax and all."

Chapter Twenty-One

When Al knocked on my door the next morning she smelled clean. She had on her new sweater and her pigtails were stiff and not fuzzy the way they get at the end of the day.

"I'm ready," she said. I could smell tooth paste like mad.

"How do you like her sweater, Mom?" I asked. I had told my mother all about it. "Isn't it nice?"

"It's lovely," my mother said. "That pink is a very good color on you. Would you like to sleep over to-night, Al?"

It was the first time I could remember my mother asking a friend of mine to sleep over. Usually I have to ask her myself and she mostly says, "I'll see," and then forgets I asked her.

"I would like to," Al said. "I have to check with my mother, though."

"Well," my mother said, "we'd like to have you. Any time."

"Thank you," Al said. "I will let you know."

We went down in the elevator and we did not talk to each other. I don't know why, except that Al was depressed. I could tell. It is very easy to get depressed when things do not happen the way you plan. People think that children do not get depressed. They think it is specially reserved for grownups. They are wrong.

"I'm glad the sun came out," Al said when we reached the basement. "It got rid of all the snow."

"Yes," I said. "That was a break."

We knocked our special knock—one, two, three, pause, then four. We waited. There was no noise at all. Unless you count the oil burner, which is always going. And the kids riding their tricycles around while their mothers did the wash. Little kids, like three or four, are very amusing. I like them. Al said once that this is because I identify with them.

"Is that good?" I had asked.

Al had shrugged her shoulders. "Good or not good, it doesn't matter. It is the way things are. Me, I don't think I was ever a child. Really a child, I mean."

I did not know what to say so I didn't say anything. I have discovered this is a good policy.

We knocked again.

"Maybe he is out," Al said.

"Where?" I said. "Where would he be? Besides, he expects us."

"Open the door," Al told me.

"Why don't you?" I said.

"All right, I will." She pushed the door open.

Mr. Richards's kitchen was very still. I could hear the refrigerator purring, sort of.

"Mr. Richards." Al looked around. "Mr. Richards."

"He must be taking a nap," I said.

Al looked at me. Mr. Richards does not take naps.

"Look in there." Al pointed to the room where Mr. Richards sleeps. It is a little closet kind of a room. He showed it to us once. You would not think it was big enough for a bedroom but he fixed it up with a bed and a radio and a chair. "All the comforts of home," he had said when he showed us around.

We tapped on the door. Then we banged. It was so quiet in there that I could hear Al's heart beating. At least I think it was hers.

Finally she opened the door. Just a crack. She looked in. "He is there," she said. "He is in bed. His eyes are closed."

"Mr. Richards," she yelled as loud as she could.

I looked over Al's shoulder and I could see him lying there, not moving. He looked awfully little.

"We'd better call somebody," I said. "I think that would be the best thing."

"Who will we call?" Al asked.

"My mother and father went downtown to look at a new couch," I said. "Your mother?" I was not telling her, I was asking.

"She has a cold. Her head is stopped up and she can't breathe. That's why she didn't go to work. She feels terrible," Al said.

"She is still your mother and we have got to call someone that we know," I said.

"All right." Al made up her mind. "If she gets mad, then she gets mad. Let's go."

When we got up to Al's apartment her mother was still in bed. She had on an old bathrobe that looked sort of like the one my mother wears, and she did not have all that stuff on her face. She looked very pale and her nose looked as though she had been blowing it a lot.

"Mom," Al said, "you have to come downstairs. It is Mr. Richards and I think something has happened to him. He is lying in bed and he does not talk to us or move."

"Mr. Richards?" Al's mother said.

"You know. He is the assistant superintendent and he is a friend of mine. Of ours. He is all alone."

Al's mother surprised me. She got up and said, "I'll have to change. I can't go down like this."

"Please," said Al. "This is urgent."

"I will call the superintendent," Al's mother said. "Maybe you children had better stay here."

"No," we said together, "he is a friend of ours."

Al's mother didn't argue. She called the super and he said he would check on Mr. Richards and see if there was anything he could do and he would call a doctor. Then we went down in the elevator and Al's mother still had her bathrobe on, so it was lucky we didn't have to stop until we got to the basement. She had a big wad of tissues in her hand. She said, "I do hope it is nothing serious," and, "I look such a fright, I hope we don't run into anyone."

Mr. Richards was just the way we had left him. We sat in the kitchen to wait. There was a big pot of soup on the stove. I was about to tell them how he made his soup when Al's mother said, "Did you ever see anything like this floor? It positively shines. I wonder how he gets such a polish."

Al sat there and the tears started running down her cheeks. They were coming fast and she did not bother to wipe them away.

"Why, Alexandra," her mother said. She took out

her wad of tissues and made a couple of swipes at Al's face. "Why, I'm sure it will be all right. Don't cry, please."

Al was really bawling by now. I had never really seen her cry before. Once she almost did when we had a fight, but mostly she gets mad and red in the face. I wanted to cry too, but I did not.

"It wasn't as easy as it looked," Al said when she could talk. "The floor. It wasn't nearly as easy as it looked."

Al's mother patted her shoulder. She said, "Oh, Al, don't cry," a couple more times. She actually called her Al.

She didn't know what Al meant. About the floor, I mean.

I was the only one who knew what she meant.

Chapter Twenty-Two

The ambulance came and took Mr. Richards away. They told us if we called the hospital in a few hours they would let us know how he was. Al and I wanted to go with him but the attendant said we were too young. So the super went, although he didn't act like he wanted to much.

We all went back to Al's apartment and her mother made cocoa, which we didn't drink. Not because it wasn't O.K. cocoa but because we didn't feel like it. I went to see if my mother and father had come back yet from shopping, but they hadn't. Teddy was there with a dopey friend of his and I didn't tell him about Mr. Richards.

I went back to Al's and we played cards while we waited. We played double solitaire and Go Fish and Al's mother tried to teach us how to play bridge. She kept patting Al on the shoulder and then she went to fix us some grilled cheese sandwiches.

"She makes delicious grilled cheese sandwiches," Al said proudly.

The doorbell rang and it was the super.

"He's had a coronary attack," he told us. "They can't say for sure what his chances are. He'll have to stay in the hospital for a while. Hope the poor old guy has all his insurance paid up."

I went down to my apartment and my mother and father had just come in. My mother started in about the beautiful couch she was thinking of buying, but I said, "Mr. Richards had a coronary attack. Al and I found him and Al's mother got the super and they took him to the hospital in the ambulance."

"Oh, dear," my mother said. "The poor man. Has he any family, anyone we should notify?"

"I don't think there's anyone to notify," I said.

Al came down a little later. "I won't be able to sleep over tonight," she said. "My mother had a dinner engagement but she broke it."

"Because of her cold?" I asked.

"That," Al said. "That and because she said she wanted to stay with me. She said she didn't want to leave me alone tonight. Actually," Al said in a confidential tone, "I didn't think it would be such a hot idea to leave her alone either. She's sort of down, you know."

"Sure," I said. "It wouldn't be much fun anyway. I'll be over in the morning and maybe we can stop at the hospital and see Mr. Richards."

"O.K." she said. "I'd better go and see if my mother wants me for anything. See you."

Chapter Twenty-Three

They said at the hospital we could visit in a couple of days. We kept calling and pestering and finally they said we could come but only stay for a few minutes. Mr. Richards was in a ward and we must remember not to talk loud or anything.

After school we went to the florist and bought him a geranium plant. Then we took the bus to the hospital and asked at the desk for his room number.

"He's in Ward D," the girl said. "Please limit your visit to five minutes."

Mr. Richards was in a room with a lot of other men. He looked awful white in the bed.

"We brought you a plant," Al said. "It's a geranium."

He said, "I never saw a prettier one. Put it here." He was there in the bed but his voice sounded like he was talking from a long way away.

I said, "How do you feel?" because I didn't know what else to say.

He smiled a little. "Everything considered, not too bad," he said. "How's things at home?"

We both stood there and said things like, "Fine, fine," and Al said she was going to polish his kitchen floor until he got back and I said I'd water his plants and then the nurse stuck her head in and said we'd better leave, visiting hours were over.

"Good-by," we said. "We'll come again in a few days."

Mr. Richards lifted his hand and let it fall. We backed out of the room. Then we stood in the hall, not doing anything.

We heard the man in the bed next to him say, "Nice couple of girls you got there. They your granddaughters?"

His voice came, faint and far away. "You might say that. Yes sir, you might say that."

We turned and walked down the hall. We rang for the elevator and went down in it and it wasn't until we got to the street that Al said, "We should've kissed him. We both should've."

"He probably knows we wanted to," I said.

We walked out into the street. It was snowing again.

Al stuck out her tongue. "It tastes like chocolate," she said.

I was tired. "Me too," I said.

Chapter Twenty-Four

Mr. Richards died in the night. He went to sleep and just never woke up. My mother says it is the best way to die.

"Look at it this way," she said. "He didn't have to suffer at all. That is all anyone can ever ask. He had a good death, a happy death. That is what I call it. Don't feel too bad."

I had never heard of a happy death. It is a new idea and I am not sure I like it or don't like it. I will have to think it over.

The funeral was just me and Al and my mother and the super. Al's mother and my father had to work. There wasn't anyone else there except a couple of old ladies who probably liked to go to funerals.

The super found an address in Mr. Richards's room that we told him was probably Mr. Richards's daughter's. He wrote her a letter telling her about Mr. Richards's death but he never heard from her.

We have a new assistant super now. He is fat and has practically no neck and he looks like he could shovel snow for three days straight. He is always shooing the little kids on their tricycles away from the laundry room and he sometimes uses foul language. I hate him and so does Al. The thing I can't stand is what Mr. Richards's kitchen floor must look like with that man living there.

It happened about a month ago, or more, maybe. Actually, it was five weeks and four days. I know because I marked the day Mr. Richards died on my calendar. I put a black circle around the day.

I must have started what Mr. Richards called growing into my bones. A boy asked me to a record hop at school. He is the creepiest boy in the whole class. But he asked me. I told him my mother wouldn't let me go.

Al has lost about a hundred pounds. She looks great. Also, her mother took her to the place she gets her hair done and had the man wash and set Al's hair and now she wears it long with a ribbon around it. It is very becoming, my mother says. She is right. But I miss Al's pigtails. I wanted her to wear it this way but now that she does I'm kind of sorry. She looks older and different, is all I know. Also her mother is going to take her on a trip at spring vacation. She is very excited about it.

I have tried skating around our kitchen floor once or twice when I was all alone in the apartment. Maybe it's because the floor is the wrong shape. It is long and narrow. Or maybe it's because I'm clumsy. But I can't do it. I just can't. The last time I tried I could almost hear Mr. Richards hollering, "Glide, glide!" and I started laughing when I remembered all the good times Al and I had with him.

That is one thing about knowing a person like Mr. Richards. You never forget. When I feel depressed I remember all the laughs we had and all the carrot sticks and the shooters of Coke, and I feel better.

My bookcase is hanging on my bedroom wall where I can see it when I wake up.

Maybe what Mr. Richards said about Al and me being stunners some day will come true. I only wish he could be around to see it happen. That's the only thing I wish.